Disney's POCAHONTAS

Adapted by
Justine Korman

Illustrated by Don Williams

A GOLDEN BOOK · NEW YORK
Western Publishing Company, Inc., Racine, Wisconsin 53404

Library of Congress Catalog Card Number: 95-75551
ISBN: 0-307-30200-8   MCMXCV

*L*isten to the voice of the wind as it tells the story
of Pocahontas, the beautiful daughter of Chief Powhatan.
Pocahontas loved the land and the many spirits that
lived in the animals, the trees, and the wind.

One day Pocahontas visited Grandmother Willow, a wise
old tree spirit. "My father wants me to marry the warrior
Kocoum," Pocahontas told her. "But he is so serious. And
lately I've been dreaming a strange dream of a spinning
arrow."

Grandmother Willow knew there was great wisdom to be
found in dreams. "It is pointing you down your path," she
told Pocahontas.

"But how do I find my path?" Pocahontas wondered.

"If you listen with your heart, you will understand," Grandmother Willow replied. "The spirits that live in all things will guide you."

So Pocahontas listened to the wind and climbed Grandmother Willow's strong branches. Off in the distance she saw some very strange clouds.

But they weren't clouds. They were the white sails of a ship bringing men from England to the New World in search of gold.

As soon as the boat touched shore, a man called John Smith climbed a tree to see the wild land. He came face-to-face with Pocahontas's friend, Meeko.

"Well, you're a strange-looking fellow!" Smith said.

John Smith had a feeling someone else was also nearby, so he hid and watched. Soon Pocahontas came into view. She was the most beautiful young woman he had ever seen! But when she saw him, Pocahontas ran to her canoe, quick as a deer. Smith ran after her.

"Don't go! Please. I won't hurt you," Smith called after her. Pocahontas could not understand the words the strange man spoke. But the sound of Grandmother Willow's words echoed in her mind. So Pocahontas listened with her heart and understood. She saw that John Smith's heart was kind.

While Pocahontas and John Smith became friends, Smith's shipmates and Pocahontas's tribe were becoming enemies! The warriors watched from the shadows as the men chopped down the trees and tore up the beautiful land. Greedy Governor Ratcliffe urged the settlers to dig faster. He wanted gold!

Then Ratcliffe's dog, Percy, spotted the Indians and yelped.

"SAVAGES! IT'S AN AMBUSH!" shrieked Ratcliffe when he saw the strange men in their buckskins. "Arm yourselves!"

Musket fire echoed through the woods like deadly thunder. A young warrior dropped to the ground with a wound in his leg.

"Namontack!" Kocoum cried as he rushed to rescue his fallen friend. "Back to the village!" Kocoum commanded.

Kocoum carried his friend home. The medicine man had never seen a wound like Namontack's. Chief Powhatan raged, "These beasts invade our shores, destroy the land . . . and now this!" He told Kocoum to send messengers to all the other Indian villages. "We will fight these dangerous strangers together," Powhatan told his people.

But even then Pocahontas was talking to her new friend, John Smith. Meeko was searching Smith's pouch for some treats but grabbed his compass instead.

"What is that?" Pocahontas asked as Meeko ran off.

"It tells you how to find your way when you are lost," Smith told her. "Meeko can keep it. I will buy another compass in London."

"London? Is that your village?" Pocahontas asked.

Smith tried to explain about cities and how his people would show hers how to build the right kind of houses and roads.

Pocahontas knew the woods around them were more beautiful than any city could ever be. So she showed John Smith her world and told him how she and her people were connected to it.

Pocahontas even took Smith to Grandmother Willow's glade. Smith was stunned. "One look at this place and the men will forget all about digging for gold."

"What is gold?" Pocahontas asked.

Smith showed her a gold coin.

"There is nothing like that around here," Pocahontas said, shaking her head.

Smith tried to tell this to Ratcliffe, but the greedy man wouldn't listen. "Those Indians have our gold and they'll do anything to keep it!" Ratcliffe shouted.

"There isn't any gold!" Smith said.

"Lies! Lies!" Ratcliffe raged. "We'll get our gold, even if we have to take it by force!"

In Powhatan's village the braves were just as eager to fight for their land. "But we don't have to fight!" Pocahontas told her father. "There must be a better path. We should try talking."

"It is clear the strangers do not want to talk," he replied.

"But if one of them did want to talk, would you listen?" Pocahontas persisted. Powhatan said yes.

That night in Grandmother Willow's glade Pocahontas said to John Smith, "Come with me and talk to my father."

Smith shook his head. "Once two sides want to fight, nothing can stop them."

"Sometimes the right path is not the easiest one," said Grandmother Willow.

Smith sighed. "All right," he said. "I'll try."

Pocahontas was so happy, she kissed him!

Meanwhile a settler named Thomas was watching them.
He had followed John Smith.

Suddenly Kocoum burst out of the woods. He had
followed Pocahontas.

"Kocoum, no!" Pocahontas cried.

But Kocoum charged at Smith. Frightened, Thomas fired
his musket and Kocoum fell. "Thomas, run!" Smith cried.

As Thomas fled, warriors swarmed into the glade. They captured John Smith and took him back to the village. "At sunrise this man will die," Chief Powhatan told his people.

Pocahontas went to Grandmother Willow. "I thought my dream led me to John Smith," she cried. "But now he is going to die! I feel so lost!"

Just then Meeko dropped a round metal object into her hands. Through her tears Pocahontas looked at John Smith's compass. The needle moved back and forth. "The spinning arrow!" she whispered.

Grandmother Willow smiled. "The arrow from your dream! It shows you your path. Let the spirits of the earth guide you."

Pocahontas ran like the wind. At dawn she reached the cliff where her father was about to carry out the sentence on John Smith.

Pocahontas threw herself across Smith's body. "If you kill him, you will have to kill me, too," she cried. "Look around you. This is where the path of hatred has brought us."

Two armies stood ready to fight. The settlers clutched their muskets. The warriors pulled their bowstrings taut.

"I love him," Pocahontas declared. "This is the path I choose, Father. What will yours be?"

Chief Powhatan dropped his weapon. "If there is to be more killing, it will not start with me."

The settlers lowered their guns.

"Now is our chance!" Ratcliffe commanded. "Fire!"

But none of the settlers would shoot. So Ratcliffe grabbed a musket and aimed at Chief Powhatan.

"No!" John Smith cried as he leaped between the bullet and its mark.

Smith had to return to England to get treatment for his wound. Ratcliffe was returning, too—in chains. Pocahontas did not go with her friend. "I am needed here," she told him.

"Wherever I am, I'll always be with you," Smith said to her as he left.

Pocahontas turned her face up to the sky. She did not cry because she knew they would always be together in their hearts.